CW00860286

I ONLY
MAKE LOVE IN
MONTRÉAL

Rabin Ramah

 FriesenPress

Suite 300 - 990 Fort St
Victoria, BC, V8V 3K2
Canada www.friesenpress.com

ISBN
978-1-5255-8238-7 (Hardcover)
978-1-5255-8239-4 (Paperback)
978-1-5255-8240-0 (eBook)

1. FICTION, SHORT STORIES (SINGLE AUTHOR)

Distributed to the trade by The Ingram Book Company

DEDICATION

*This book is
dedicated to
everyone
who
reads
it.*

TABLE OF CONTENTS

LAWRENCE

Lawrence, Lawrence did you wash your ass this morning?"
Tanti Baby screamed from the middle of the *savannah*.
"Lawrence, Lawrence! Did you hear me? Lawrence, a
calling ya!"

Tanti Baby was screaming at Lawrence from a distance.
Lawrence was walking and kept on walking. Make believing
he didn't hear Tanti. Pretending he didn't hear Tanti.

"Lawrence, a talking to ya," she screamed again.
"Lawrence, ya want me to cut your sass this morning?" She
screamed to deaf ears.

Lawrence stopped in his tracks and turned his head
towards the orange figure in the middle of the savannah.

"Lawrence, answer me now," she called. "Lawrence, did
you wash your ass this morning?"

"Yesses!" he sang to her from the distance

"Wait till you get home, I'll be waiting for ya!" she cried

"Girl, leave the child alone," Mame said to Tanti.

"Lawrence, go to school," Mame shouted at him. "Girl,
way you do that to the child for?" she asked Tanti.

"Lawrence, go to school," Mame shouted again.

"Girl, he shits his pants yesterday and walked around all day smiling. He come home and hide the pants under the bed," Tanti answered Mame.

As Lawrence walked, he tried to hide among the rest of the children hurrying to school with their nicely pressed uniforms, but Tanti saw him. Lawrence knew that when he got home, he was going to get it for trying to hide from his Mame for shitting his pants, but more for ignoring her screaming.

A day didn't go by without Lawrence getting lashed for something, but this morning was especially bad. Tanti Baby was looking for him. She was mad because she had to take the cow out. Uncle was sick, so she was left to tie the cow by herself. If she didn't believe the kids should get a good education, she would have made Lawrence stay home and do it.

Mame and Tanti Baby lived a fair distance from each but was still considered neighbours. Mame lived closer to the savannah with the best grass for grazing the cow. From the middle of the savannah, in front of Mame's house, Tanti Baby saw Lawrence trying to hide in the school line. As she looked up from tying the cow, the children all heard her scream, "That mother ass, bet ya he didn't wash his ass this morning!"

Mrs. Armstrong followed the line of children with finely pressed khaki pants and blue, short-sleeve tops to school.

Lawrence was praying to God that Tanti Baby did not say anything else. He followed the line of school children along the white gravel road, and as he walked, the line got longer and longer as the uniformed children marched to school. By seven-thirty the children's paths were filled with an ant line as they thought of the strap if they were late. The students were from Standard One to Standard Five. They were all Roman Catholics.

Mrs. Armstrong followed the line, keeping a silent eye on everyone. Mrs. Armstrong was the Standard One teacher and pitch black; she was respected and feared because of the whip she carried. Even on the weekends the school children were frightened of her. Feeling the presence of Mrs. Armstrong behind them, the students hurried along to school, ignoring Lawrence.

"Girl, why did you do that to the boy?" Mame asked Tanti Baby. Mame hid behind the giant doors in the quarters, hoping Lawrence wouldn't see her laughing.

"He have no shame whatsoever," Tanti Baby said. "Wait till he gets home; he'll have to wash all that shit out of his pants."

"You didn't have to embarrass the child like that," Mame said to Tanti.

"Look, girl, I have to get up early to tie the cow this morning. This means milking and walking the cow to the savannah. That man is sick, and I am going to the twelve-thirty today," Tanti Baby replied.

Tanti, Mame, and a few of the ladies from the village went to the twelve-thirty every Thursday. Thursdays was the new releases from India. *Bobby* was playing at the Reno and the Metro. The same movie never played at the same cinemas at the same time.

"Look, Baby is taking the cow to the savannah. Baby, where you going, girl? What happened to the children? What the matter with Uncle?" They called one question after another as Baby Tanti passed with the cow.

"Look, shut your ass and don't bother may," Baby Tanti shouted back. She pulled the cow to follow her as the cow mooed in resistance.

The neighbours laughed and laughed as she passed by with the cow. "Baby? You can't wear high heels to take the cow out," the neighbours shouted after her.

By the time she travelled two blocks, pulling the cow with resistance, the whole neighbourhood was out looking to see what the commotion was about. Baby Tanti was dressed in an orange taffeta dress with high heels and red lipstick. Her hair was pinned up, and all of this was to take the cow to the savannah.

Baby Tanti was big. But even the size she was, Baby Tanti was sexy. She liked hearing the whistles as she walked by on her way to the twelve-thirty. This morning it was the cow. Baby Tanti ignored the questions and remarks. She wasn't afraid to bust a good cuss on their asses. Everyone said she had a nasty mouth and wasn't afraid to use it. She didn't care; she couldn't or care less.

Mame was one of the very few that liked Baby Tanti. When Baby Tanti moved to the village, Mame and her never talked, but one day Baby Tanti came over crying with blue marks on her face and arms. Ever since, they got along. Baby Tanti told her about the seven children; she had them one after another. Lawrence was the oldest, and according to Tanti, the laziest—"children are lazy that wants to play."

No one was sure how Baby Tanti was feeling about her children. She was always whipping someone's ass.

"Who is crying?"

"Do you want to cry some more?"

"The more you cry, the more you will taste the belt."

Mame and the ladies saw Baby Tanti every Thursday for the twelve-thirty at the Reno or the Metro and for supper. She walked around the savannah. It was the long way to Mame's house—the long way meant more admiring eyes. Every Thursday was a new dress, or Sunday for a wedding.

Baby Tanti was good for the news. Who was dead and who was getting married and a new baby? But one thing she was known for was the movies. Baby Tanti saw every movie first. She was upset if you saw the movie before her.

By the time they all reached the Metro Cinema, the line was long and heading up the street. Everyone was dressed to the nines. This was the biggest movie out of India, starring Rishi Kapoor and Dimple Kapadia. The biggest scandal: Dimple wore a bikini in the movie. The lineup was men, and men and women. No one could stop talking about Dimple.

Baby Tanti didn't like waiting, and she didn't wait. She would clear everybody out of the way and move up to the ticket wicket. The ticket man, when seeing Tanti, would show teeth from ear to ear. Pitch-black skin and gleaming white teeth.

"Baby, a got your ticket," he said to her.

She returned the smile and answered, "Right, boy."

The ticket man gave her three balcony tickets. Baby Tanti loved a great smile. He had a great smile. They started talking, ignoring the growing line. When they finished, the ticket man escorted Baby Tanti, Mame, and Aunt Dolly to the balcony, with much disapproval from the women waiting in line.

"Aye, aye, you own the cinema?" the line shouted at Baby Tanti.

Baby Tanti shouted back, "Do you want a good cuss?"

The people in the line turned to silence, with dumb-founded looks on their faces.

"Then shut your ass and wait."

"Girl, why must you talk like that?" Mame asked Tanti.

"Girl, I am just having fun," Baby Tanti responded.

"Baby? Do you have to talk like that?" Aunt Dolly questioned. "This is why I don't like coming out with you," she continued.

"Dolly, I didn't ask for your company!" Baby Tanti lashed back.

Mame's name was Baby. They called her Baby because she was tiny. She was below five feet, and small at that. Baby Tanti got her name because she was bigger than a heifer and smaller than a cow. Now, Aunt Dolly was a different story. She was dry and sour in her looks and attitude. Our nannies were old, and whether bitter and ugly, we had to show respect and a funeral every week. Baby Tanti got her name from being fat from years of uncontrollable eating of sweets. That was one way to stop a crying Baby. For breakfast, lunch, and dinner, sweets were it. But Baby Tanti was the best. She never thought about her weight and didn't care who thought she was fat.

For such a heavy-set woman, Baby Tanti could dance. She had old-world moves. She had a reputation from village to village. Men loved her and women hated her.

"I can get any man I want and out-dance any woman any day, anytime," she would say with a laugh. At the weddings, the young women would dance, but nothing could beat Baby Tanti's moves. Men and women would stop to look.

Auntie Dolly always talked behind Baby Tanti's back, always in reference to a heifer.

Baby Tanti loved the fact everyone was afraid—except Mame.

When Mame arrived in the village, she moved in with a garden, cows, chickens, ducks, geese, goats, and fields of crops. When Baby Tanti arrived at the village, the house was bare and falling: the yard was overgrown with grass and bushes. The galvanized steel roof was falling, and there was a big hole in the living room looking down onto the dirt floor. The bedroom doors were off their hinges and slapped to one side. The kitchen had no running water, and the stove was rusted through. The coconut trees reached into the house, the window had no glass, their wooden latches hanging from one hinge, and the flooring was being devoured by moss after neglect. The flooring needed new gobar from the fields and red mud from the river.

That was when it all started. On the same day she arrived, before she unpacked, she gathered her things and went back to her father's house. She told Uncle if he ever wanted to see her again, the place would have to be cleaned. That very same night, Tanti Baby's father and mother bought Baby Tanti back to the house. Everyone called him Nana and her mother Nane. The crying was not just tears; it was bawling and wailing. Baby Tanti was well cared for in her father's house. Cleaning was something she did not know.

Nana stood in silence as Nane cried. He got out of the car and opened the door and grabbed her suitcase and dropped it by the gate. Baby Tanti got out of the car. Nana got back in the car and drove off, not looking back. Baby Tanti stood by the gate as Nana and Nane drove off. That night, the house was in chaos. No one slept in the county from all the noise coming from Uncle's house. By morning, the kitchen and living room looked somewhat decent.

Baby Tanti was extremely popular in the county. But there were those that were jealous. Baby Tanti was sexy, and with sexy went with a reputation. She was a strong-willed woman. No one interfered with the quarrelling when it started at the house. Everyone learned in the county to mind their own business when it came to man and wife. Uncle would start with his drunken cussing, and Tanti would not hesitate to beat him. The fighting was over the children. Too many children. All boys.

Lawrence was the oldest and responsible for looking after the rest of his brothers. Ravi was second, and Moco Plantain was the third. The last two were unnoticeable. Quiet was their names.

Moco Plantain was unusually small, so everyone nicknamed him Moco Plantain after the fruit. The nickname stuck.

Baby Tanti always wanted a girl but had all boys. She was sad when the last boy appeared.

Lawrence's father worked in the cane fields. It was back-breaking work. They had a bull and a cow. The bull pulled the cart with Uncle, and the cow was out in the fields during the day.

Lawrence looked after his brothers. Baby Tanti would not clean up after any of the boys. She just refused. Uncle found out it was like talking to a brick wall.

Moco was sweet. We saw a lot of him. He appeared exactly at supper. No one asked why he was there, but he took his place at the table. We ate on green plantain leaves. We grew them in the back yard by the ravine. We also grew dashine leaves and eddoes. We cooked outside in a dirt fire side. We never asked Moco why he was there at supper, and we never assumed anything. It was something we just didn't do. Lawrence and Uncle knew where he was in the evenings.

Baby Tanti loved Mame's cooking. Even dal and rice tasted amazing. Mame was known for her roti. Baby Tanti's favourite roti was curried chicken and potatoes.

Baby Tanti would yell, "Your uncle cannot cook dal and bath."

There was no table or chairs; we all sat on the dirt floor, which was cleaned and swept every day. We all ate with our hands. We had short stoop chairs that were painted with the colours of our house. They were used by the adults in the family.

Baby Tanti would sit on the stoop with her legs crossed. The wind was a gentle breeze. Tanti would look happy when you were looking. Her smile was heaven.

Then, in quiet moments, sadness would fall. With the food on her lap, her thoughts would disappear in the distance as the great sadness enveloped her. Tears would quietly flow from her eyes. Mame would sit beside her and hold her hands as the tears came pouring out. Mame and Tanti had secrets. Secrets only they knew.

Baby Tanti hated her life. Life was not supposed to be like this. She never wanted to get married. This marriage was arranged and forced. She never wanted children. But they were here, and Uncle would have to help look after them. She spent most of the time at Mame's house. If Uncle needed to find her, he would send one of the boys.

We loved Baby Tanti. She was a lot of fun. She would make us laugh from tickling. We would be tickled until we cried for her to stop. We did not remember that she had children of her own. Moco was quiet, so we didn't notice him.

Mame was busy with cooking, sewing, the crops, washing. The day didn't stop, but Baby Tanti and Mame were best friends. At night, she would leave for her own house in the pitch of darkness.

Lawrence used to make believe he was the only child. He used to tell everyone that he was adopted. He looked exactly like Baby Tanti. Very fair skinned. Lawrence's house was near the edge of a ravine that flows to the Couva River. The house was normal. It took years to build from one room to six rooms. The main floor had a kitchen and an opening sitting area. Concrete stilts were holding the second floor up. The eating area was just a long table and two long benches on either side. There was a place for Baby Tanti and Moco.

The ground was hard with pasted red clay and dirt. It was nice to walk on with bare feet but became muddy during the rainy season. The yard was surrounded with all kinds of fruit trees—coconut, ferns, dashine, plantain, four different kind of mangoes, avocado. Soursup, sugar apples, guava, and a patch of cane. The dashine plants and cassava lined the ravine. This was a normal backyard for the size of the house. In the middle of the backyard was a small temple to honour the Lord Vishnu. Like all the other houses, the latrine was built towards the end of the property to give privacy. The difference between Mame's house and Baby Tanti's was that she had electricity and running water. We had to go to the water tap on the main street to collect buckets of water before we rushed off to school.

The steps leading to the upper gallery were painted red, along with the floor. The walls were a cream yellow, the roof a vibrant green. This was a very modest house. As the boys appeared, the house got larger and the land got smaller. Uncle worked in the cane fields and then worked at home when they needed more room. The beds were made from dry coconut husk.

Ravi was the bed wetter. The coconut husk would rot. It was hard changing the husk when it was not in season. All the children collected the coconuts to husk and make oil. Baby Tanti did not collect the coconuts.

Lawrence hated school like we all did. He was one of the most lashed students. There were days when we could not sit. He was lashed on his ass for sleeping. Trying to help him would mean lashes for us as well.

Mr. Dachawan taught Standard Four. We were five to a desk. It was cramped. There were close to fifty students in the classroom, and Mr. Dachawan ran the class with a whip. He enjoyed beating the blackboard when he wanted to make a point. The sound would wake us up. A jolt of fright would strike through our bodies like lightning. Mr. Dachawan did not care about the chores Lawrence had to do before school. During recess, Lawrence looked for his brothers to make sure they were not being bullied by the older kids.

Lawrence heard his mother calling him from the distance as he followed the line of blue-and-khaki uniformed children to school. The thunder of her voice reached his ears. The sound of his name sang, the ringing echoed into the centre of his head. Lawrence, stripped of his dignity, froze as both sides of his head thundered with his name. The moment he heard his name, he could have pissed his pants. His bowels moved to the exit of his pants as he tightened the grip on the refuse waiting to soil his pants. The pain grew the faster he walked. He wished he was alone. He heard laughter from everyone. The laughter was thunder in his head. The eyes staring and laughing. Lawrence was alone in the line, and he was lonely. The darkness crept up around him. He wanted to die. He prayed for the darkness to cover him because he knew that he would be safe. The darkness would hide him from the eyes and laughter. Fingers pointing, the humiliation grew.

Lawrence woke up late because he was out playing in the savannah with the rest of the boys kicking around a ball the night before. Lawrence didn't pay attention to the setting sun. He forgot about the cow in the middle of the savannah. By the time he remembered the cow had to be brought to the shed for the night, he was ready to go home. The cow had not seen Lawrence for hours. She started crying as the sun was setting. She could always tell time. Once she saw

Lawrence coming towards her, she stopped crying, happy to see a familiar shadow.

Lawrence hugged her and scratched her behind her ears. She was happy. He untied her rope, and she ran across the savannah towards the house. Lawrence chased her before she reached the road. If she got run over, he might as well be dead. If she reached home before he did, he would be dead. He ran and caught the rope and slowed her down. He patted her, and she calmed down. She was just tired and would feel better in her pen.

He called her "Mama."

"It's okay, Mama," he said as he lovingly stroked her to calm her down. She didn't like being out this late. She felt safer in her pen. The sky was starting to fill with bats. Bats were everywhere. The mosquitoes were starting to bite.

When he finally reached home, none of the chores were done. The buckets of rainwater were empty. The smaller boys were already asleep, having hardly anything to eat.

Uncle was still at the canteen. Baby Tanti was still at Mame's. He was lucky he reached home first. He found a bucket of water and quickly washed his face. Mama found her way to her shed. He tried to make the place look clean. The moon was already over the house. He looked at the pile of dirty dishes and food thrown all over the dirt floor, swore at Vishnu, and went off to bed. Ravi and his brothers were sleeping in his bed. He crawled into bed with his brothers.

He heard the gate open as Uncle stumbled into the yard. He prayed that Uncle would leave them alone tonight. Uncle climbed the steps to the gallery, falling onto his face, and he didn't move for what seemed likes ages.

Lawrence whispered "hush" to his brothers. He could see the fright in their eyes.

Uncle finally got up and moved into the living room and fell onto the couch. Lawrence covered his brothers' mouths to stifle their cries. He told them to sleep.

With Baby Tanti's voice ringing in his head, he froze in mid step. Courage came, and he kept on walking.

"Lawrence, did you wash your ass this morning?" she screamed again. Lawrence wanted to cry. He wanted to run and hide, but where? Lawrence wanted to die.

Mrs. Armstrong was there beside him. She could hear his mother screaming, and he kept on walking. All the children turned around to look at Lawrence, not at Baby Tanti screaming from the distance. Mrs. Armstrong stood with her black face frozen. Her school bag was held tightly to her side. She slowly turned her head to look at the middle of the savannah. Baby Tanti was dressed in orange taffeta. Baby Tanti was waving at Mrs. Armstrong.

She raised her right hand and returned the greeting. Mrs. Armstrong stared at Baby Tanti. The things she wanted to say to her. She looked at Lawrence and her eyes filled with tears. Tears that she stifled back. Mrs. Armstrong knew what Lawrence was feeling. She could feel his world destroyed. She felt for Lawrence. She felt hate for Baby Tanti. If she could, she would have given the strap to Baby Tanti. She looked at Lawrence with pity. She wanted to take Lawrence away from this moment. Embarrassed for him, Mrs. Armstrong marched on to school, ignoring the destruction of Lawrence. Today, he would be left alone to heal his wounds.

"Lawrence, did you wash your ass this morning?" rang through her ears as she walked to school. She could still hear the laughter from the students. But this wasn't funny.

"Lawrence, Lawrence," she cried in her head.

"Lawrence, did you wash your ass this morning?" There was laughter. The laughter was coming from the students of his school. Lawrence did not have many friends. Mrs. Armstrong was directly behind Lawrence. The laughter stopped when the students saw Mrs. Armstrong. The laughter was in his head. It was a loud chorus.

Lawrence stopped; time froze in steps. He heard his mame. He stopped and turned around. He was alone in that moment. He turned round and shouted, "Yes, Mame!"

He continued to walk to school without breaking the line. The look was frozen on Lawrence's face. He looked at no one. He ignored the call of his name.

Shamed, Lawrence walked to school with the back of his pants hardening, the waste drying to his bottom. Everyone was staring at his behind. Some of the kids were clenching their noses with two fingers and pointing at Lawrence.

Lawrence screamed yes to his Mame because he knew if he did not answer that when he got home tonight the belt would be waiting for him. Lawrence did wash his ass that morning. Last night he had hidden his pants under the bed, hoping not to forget them in the morning. Baby Tanti had found them from the smell.

Lawrence sat in the middle of the bench in the back row. The class was fifty-five heads. Mr. Dachawan would walk up the middle row with a big Tambrand stick slapping the side of his leg. He made sure there was fear in all of us. There were ten words in our mental test, which was a spelling test. Each wrong word was a lash on your behind. Ten words wrong was on your knuckles, open palm, and your behind. The girls got it across their hands. We all sat straight as needles with bent necks writing on a straight line. We dared not glance over to another student's paper. We listened carefully.

Lawrence sat in the middle of the desk, sandwiched between four kids. In the middle of the spelling test, he felt it. His bowels moved. It was still an hour before recess. Mr. Dachawan was repeating the words, pacing the centre aisle. Lawrence closed his eyes and prayed. His breathing became faster, thinking that would stop his bowels from moving. The pressure built in his bottom. He was sweating from head to toe. His back was soaking wet as he shits his pants on the bench. He never felt better than to have that relief. Mr. Dachawan did not notice the smell coming from the back of the class. His fellow students could not stomach the smell but could not say anything. They were too frightened to move.

Lawrence sat still as the bell rang for recess. He got up, took his position in the line, and marched out the door to the playground. He ran to the far end of the playground to look for a corner to hide until the bell rang again. He removed his pants and grabbed some leaves and wiped his bottom with them. He scraped the shit from his pants. At three o'clock, he grabbed his brothers and sent them home. He forgot about his pants and ran to the savannah to play.

Lawrence's skin was light. Smooth complexation. High cheekbones. His hair was pitch black and soaking with coconut oil. He stared at you with piercing black eyes. His school uniform was starched and pressed, and he had white polished shoes. His uniform hid his hungry stomach.

Lawrence was nine.

I HAVE SEEN THE LIGHT

I have seen the Light
And I closed my eyes
To see the Darkness
To walk safely through the Light.

Running towards the Light
To destroy the Light
To break the Light
To stab the Light

Eyes shut tight
I see the Darkness
No Boundaries for the Light.

DOGLA

Mrs. Johnson lived just behind the abattoir. Her children grown and married and free. It was painted green and blue from the outside. The roof was covered in galvanized steel like everybody else's. No one knew what the inside looked like because no one was invited. No stranger could enter the grounds. There were two storeys of steep stairs leading up to the second floor from the outside, with no guard rail. The house was built to withstand full-force winds, floods, and hurricanes during the rainy months.

We called everything by season. Rainy season, mango season, cane season. Her house, from a distance, was no different from the rest of the neighbourhood. They all looked the same except for the size of the property and height of the house and the manicured lawns. Her house was built on the best land, with easy access to water from the river. It also had one of the largest bananas and mango fields.

The fence surrounding the property was wire-weaved like diamonds. Easy to climb. At the top of the fence it jutted out forward with barbed wire. To get over the fence would take some skill. Along the perimeter we found a hole made by the dogs. We watched this hole to see how much bigger it was getting.

The house was just behind the abattoir with a wall of mango trees. The abattoir did its slaughter only on Saturdays. The smell of pig shit and the squealing of the pigs did not bother Mrs. Johnson.

Mrs. Johnson was the meanest person in the neighbourhood. She was pitch black. She stayed far away from the Coolies in the neighbourhood. The fruits would be ripening on the trees. The laden branches would be touching the ground. The high winds and rain would come and blow the mangoes off the trees. Juicy, ripe mangoes and guava would be rotting on the ground, pommes setay would be splitting open on the branches, bananas were turning black, birds were pecking and eating their fill, plantain trees were falling to the ground. Mrs. Johnson would not share.

She had two black Dobermans to guard the property. No one could pass close to the property without the dogs barking to stay away. They paraded the property night and day.

No one had seen her or cared to look for her. The curtains were drawn. The house was always in darkness. They called her a "sookoonya." They said she came out at night. She did have the most beautiful trees around. Her mangoes were the best. They were big and juicy. We would make bets to see who was brave enough to go and thief the mangoes. Sometimes after school a gang of us would walk past the house with whitewashed rocks and throw them at the dogs. The dogs would attack the fence, snarling and growling at us. The dogs would wake Mrs. Johnson. From the second floor she would scream, "I am going to tell your mothers!"

We all ran, laughing. We all heard something different. We all heard the curse. It was a curse. We ran home and told everyone what we heard. Each was a different story.

Sure enough, by the time we got home, Mame would know. Mr. Badbolall was waiting. We got lix on our ass and we could not sit. We went off to bed with no food.

Next day we had high winds, heavy rains. The mangoes, the guava, the pommes setay, the breadfruit, the jacknut, the zaboca would all be on the ground. I smiled to myself. Mrs. Johnson's yard would be covered in fruit. The fruit we were not allowed to pick, the fruit we were not allowed to taste. I always imagined she would eat till she was fat and exploded. There would be more than enough for the birds and us. The greedy Mrs. Johnson. That stingy old nigger. That nasty sookoonya. I will be waiting for you, Mrs. Johnson, sitting high on top of the tree looking down on we, we pea.

It was coming towards the end of crop season. Her bad Obeah did not work. It was hot. By noon we would all have to be inside. The trees were dry, and the ground was hard and cracked under our bare feet as we walked in the hot sun. No one invited us in to cool off. We knew better than to be out in the noon sun. All the stores were shut until 3:00 p.m.

We passed Mrs. Johnson's house. As usual, the curtains were drawn. We did not hear the dogs. Those devil dogs, they were probably dead. Maybe got hit by lightning? We said things just to say things. The heat was unbearable. Our skin was getting black as pitch. This was the price of greed.

We waited, I listened. We heard no dogs. I rattled the fence with a dry piece of wood. No devil dogs came charging towards the fence to devour us. Looking up to the second floor, we saw no sign Mrs. Johnson's loud curse. We stared through the fence. Rows and rows of manicured trees. Standing straight. Tops green. The larger leaves dried as kindling. The banana leaves dropped to the trunk of the trees. We all stared. We all stared at the fruit dropping from the trees. The ground covered in rotten, bird-pecked mangoes, pommes setay, rotten plantain. As I climbed the fence, the rest of the kids tried to pull me down. I kicked them. At the top, I listened, but still no barking. Two of the boys grabbed me and said, "The hole."

The hole was bigger now. I could easily crawl under.

"Where are the dogs?" I asked.

I crawled under the fence. It still was not easy, but I got through. I lay still on the ground. Covered in dust. Everyone stayed still, staring into the trees. No dogs. I got up and slowly walked towards the trees. I grabbed mangoes and tossed them over the fence. Still no dogs. Everyone collected the mangoes as I tossed them. They were all happy. They were jumping for joy. I had to tell them to stop. I whispered for them to run. "Go home now."

Covered in dirt, I looked around the yard. The trees were dry. Leaves brown, fruits covering the ground, half-eaten by the birds. Dog shit everywhere.

As I pulled the box of matches out of my pocket, the dead silence was deafening. The trees stopped rustling; the breeze stopped blowing. I was alone, standing in the middle of the fig trees. I took the match out and I heard the lightning as I struck the match and touched each fig tree with the flames. The sky darkened.

The flames rushed upwards into the Caribbean sky. The sky darkened red, and orange flames danced upwards. I stood and watched as the flames moved towards me. I feel the heat. The heat wanting me. I could not blink. I heard the crack of branches falling. The wind picked up, fanning the flames. The flames rushed through the orchard, burning everything to ashes. The black ashes sailed in the air and landed gently on the ground. Tree to tree, the flames roared like thunder and reached the house.

The sky opened and the rain poured out. The sound was deafening. I ran towards the fence and crawled through the hole. I ran and ran until I reached the cane fields. I ran into the field until I could run no more. I sat in the row of dry stalks. I hid until I thought it was safe to come out. The rain stopped. I looked at the sky. It was blue again. I heard the deafening sound again and ignored it. I got up and walked out of the cane field and slowly walked home. The sky was blue, and black ashes gently floated around me. I put my hands out to catch them.

Mrs. Johnson passed two years later. Mame knew before she passed. The sun was shining. The sky was Caribbean blue. Like any normal day. Then, out of the blue, the rain started to fall. Everyone in the village came out to look at the sky. The rain looked like falling diamonds. Everyone waited for the news.

Mrs. Johnson was Catholic. She would be buried. They were taking her to the Catholic cemetery by the sea. A long black hearse slowly rolled by the house. Mame called for us to come inside. As the hearse passed by, we all bit and whipped our fingers to ward off the curse of Mrs. Johnson. The slow procession followed the hearse. Around twenty-four men followed the hearse, all dressed in pitch-black long jackets and black pants, wearing top hats. Their faces were pitch black. We could only see the whites of their eyes. They were all like tall bamboo sticks painted with the pitch of night. Walking behind the hearse in a slow, even pace, I took deeper bites into my fingers just to make sure Mrs. Johnson's curse didn't work. We didn't need anyone in the procession to know the story. Rumours would fly by sundown.

Someone was looking at me. Directly into me. Eyes piercing, cutting into my soul. The stare was blinding. I couldn't see, but a white light reached into my head, slicing my mind into hurting pieces. I felt helpless with all my guards let down. This man was looking directly into my soul, he was pulling me apart. I couldn't move. I stood frozen.

It took forever for the hearse to pass by. The procession was slow. It was around five o'clock when the march arrived in front of the church, which was slate grey with wooden blinds and burgundy frames and made of wood. The main entrance tower pointing to God was over six storeys high with wooden shuttered windows all the way up. The church shutters were always closed. For that matter, any windows were closed.

Just above the entrance the white Jesus was hung on a cross, looking down as you entered for morning pray. Beside the entrance was a marble stand with a bowl to hold the holy water. The church doors weighed a ton, with a giant steel latch to keep the thieves and the homeless and the beggars out at night. To the west and east wings, stained-glass windows lined the walls telling the story of Christ who came to save my soul. He died for my sins.

The main hall had orderly wooden pews made of the finest wood from the county; the county gave the best. The ceiling was like looking up into heaven with all the stars in the sky. The altar was raised and simple, with a wooden cross and a stained-glass star. As the sun climbed into the sky, the sun beamed through the star and lit the altar. The white Father would tell us our sins and ask us for money to cleanse our souls so we could all go to heaven. The church looked menacing from the distance, especially during the rainy season.

Mrs. Johnson was not taken into the church for service. The burial plots were just in front of the church. The British and the Spanish were there. The cemetery was covered in white stone crosses on the spot. Mrs. Johnson did not have a cross; she had a grey headstone. Most of the graves were overgrown with weeds. You could tell where they were going to put Mrs. Johnson, as it was the plot that was freshly dug. The dirt that came out of the earth was black and wet. The coffin was a smooth, shiny black with silver handles. Mrs. Johnson had four pallbearers to carry her coffin. No one said anything as Mrs. Johnson was lowered into the ground. No one cried. No flowers. Just stone silence. Twenty-four men and one woman. The one woman wore white gloves and a black veil over her head. Two men stood with shovels.

Where was the priest to say a prayer for Mrs. Johnson? The church was silent. It stood pitch black in silence. The clock struck six, and the bells did not toll, and no candles were lit.

I came to see Mrs. Johnson in the ground—to make sure she was in the ground. I did not leave until the caretakers finished shovelling the last dirt on the mound. The time was past six o'clock, and the blue Caribbean sky had long disappeared for the night. I was alone with Mrs. Johnson. I stared at the mound. We both were silent. The tombstone was only plain. Just "Mrs. Johnson" and no date.

I will remember you, Mrs. Johnson, and you will remember me; I am sure we will see each other again. If not soon.

I have taken the walk from the beach for years, but this night seemed to take longer. The shadows along the way created by the light of the moon were of trees dancing in the night. The breeze was swaying the branches back and forth. Mrs. Johnson was buried on a good night.

Mrs. Johnson, you are a fool. Indeed, you are. You should have been cremated. Cremated on a bed of pitch pine. Bathed in sandalwood perfume and dressed in white muslin and laid upon the pyre. If you had a son, he would light the sulphur on your lips and set the pyre on fire. The flames would consume you fast. The flames would rise, and the perfume would travel with the wind that would carry you where you were free.

In the morning, your son would come and take you, he would take a heavy hammer and smash your head. Collect your ashes and bones and give you to the sea, where you would swim free with life, or he would put you in an urn and sit you on the mantle to worship you. He would throw you to the wind and have you fly across the sky. You could be hurricanes or waves slapping the rocks on the beach.

But you are Catholic. You are six feet under, where you will rot, and the worms will eat you. No one will remember you like everybody else where overgrown grass will win. There is no worship for your headstone. Your grave will be robbed for your gold. But the fools that will dig you up will find out there was no gold and leave you in an open grave.

I smiled to myself and kept on walking, ignoring the breeze whistling in the trees and the bird screaming, "Mrs. Johnson."

"Um, someone might as well cry," I thought to myself

By the time I got home, Mame was out looking for me, and she saw me coming up the road. I only saw her dark silhouette standing under the moonlight, with her hands on her hips. The moon cast a protective light over her head. I knew it was her. Her hair was blowing in the night wind. It was pitch black and passing her knee. Her hair has a life of its own. It was a curse to cut your hair in my family. At night we would sit and comb out the knots while we heard stories from India.

The wind was taking her hair into the night sky, playing with her. Mame usually had her hair tied in a bun. For it to be this loose meant it was late. Her hands were on her hips as she waited. Hands on hips meant Mame was upset.

I decided not to say a word. What would be would be. As I got closer, I noticed Mr. Badbolall on her left side. I walked right past her. She followed me silently. I feel her stare on the back of my head. I went straight to the latrine, then the shower and into bed. No food.

The house was on stilts but only five steps high. When the fires came, and the floods, it was easier to escape. We lived in a long house, and all the bedrooms were connected. The only room that was not connected was the latrine and the shower. They were at the far end of the lot near the ravine. We had no electricity, so we had to be in before dark.

We all had posies made from English porcelain. In the morning we each had to empty and clean the posies. Luxury to piss and shit in. We could not leave the house at night to use the latrine. In the pitch night, gunshots were heard in the distance.

Mame woke us up at two in the morning. Sleepy eyed and tired, we got up and stumbled out of bed. We didn't say a word. She told us to be quiet. The dogs were awake and followed us to the savannah. The moon showed us the way. We passed the jacknut tree in the backyard and crossed the ravine. Passed the abattoir and walked into the savannah.

There it was. We all looked up at the sky, an indescribable picture of a billion stars. We lay on the savannah grass and stared at the sky. It was our present from Mame. We could not count. The stars blinked. We reached our hands up to the sky to try and touch the sky. The stars blinked. We tired ourselves out and headed back to bed.

There was something about those nights. It is as if we will never see them again. We will never be together again. We picked our stars and named them for ourselves.

We were up at the cock's crow and into the cold shower. If you weren't up before, you would be now. Our uniforms were neatly pressed with starch. Before breakfasting, we were off to church for six o'clock. By 6:45 a.m. we were home for breakfast, plain roti and fried eggs with a cup of black tea in a white enamel cup. By eight o'clock we were all at school, waiting in line for uniform inspection.

"Come sing a song,
sing a beautiful song,
come here where the raindrops fall, the days are bright,
shine all around us day and by night,
Jesus, the light of the world."

ROTI

Nigger, Nigger, come for Roti
All the Roti done.
When the Coolies raise the Guns, all the Niggers run.

SWEET TAMBRAND WHIP

Big Teeth, Big Mouth
Big Eyes, Big Nose, Big Lips
Big Ears, Black Face, Black Lips
Dogla, Nigger, Coolie, Paki
Last in gym
Last in class
Lix on my hands, Lix on my ass
Lix in the morning, lix in the afternoon
Dunce
Battyboy, Battyman
Common Entrance, 45 out of 50.

Spelling Test was called Mental Test. With each answer wrong, you will get the lashes on your ass or on your hands. Depends on how dark you are. You can get it on your knuckles or on the palm of your hands.

School was Roman Catholic. We all wore starched, pressed uniforms, had manicured fingernails, whitewashed crepe soles and washed hair, a crew cut or tied to keep out of our face.

We all had to say, "Good morning," "Good evening" to our teachers and headmaster. We never called them by their names. It was Miss or Sir. If you did make that mistake, it was the straps or the whip. This included the weekends. If your teacher could not find the whip, you would be sent to the headmaster to explain what you did, and he would give you the whip.

Yes? A whip, a Tambrand whip. It was a hot whip, and it better be a good whip, a stinging whip, a painful whip, a cutting whip, your whip, a burning, piercing, you-do-not-cry whip.

You were sent to find your own whip, a long-scaled whip, white-bark whip, white-pain blinding whip. You were shaking while you looked for your whip. You didn't want a dry whip, a cracking whip, you wanted a green whip. No-knots-in-the-branch whip. You know what would happen if you brought back a thick whip.

Time? Too much time looking for your snake whip. Time is more lix.

Mary stood with her hands in prayer as I looked for the Tambrand tree in the church garden. She stared at me. I stared back. I didn't say a prayer because Mary could not help me.

I found the Tambrand tree. I looked at it, and the branches were high. I jumped with my outstretched hands to grab a branch and pull it down to break a piece. I couldn't jump high enough. I had to climb the tree. The Tambrand tree had a dark bark covering the whip inside her branches. I climbed the tree and broke a branch. Threw it to the ground and stayed on the tree for a few minutes before I climbed down.

I climbed down and broke another piece off the broken branch. I scaled the whip with my bare fingers. The bark peeled off easily, showing the white whip inside. I sliced the air with it, making a whooshing sound. It cut the air in half.

As I marched back to the schoolhouse, I felt Mary looking at me. I passed the front of the church and Jesus looked down at me, but there was dead silence as he stared.

As I reached the school, the students were staring at me. I walked up the stairs into the main hallway and marched to the headmaster's office. There was dead silence as I walked towards the back of the school. I felt every eye on me. Teachers smiled.

There were no classrooms. The school was one big room separated by wooden blackboards. The ceiling was high, with wooden beams crossing all the way through, covered in galvanized steel. Nothing was more beautiful than the sound of the falling rain on the galvanized steel. The floors were made of thick planks. The desk was five to a bench. Classes were Standard One to Standard Five.

I reached the headmaster's office. The door was open. I stood there until he saw me and got up and took the whip from me. He sliced the air in front of him with the whip. The whip made a cracking sound. The whip cut the air in half. I stood there, stone faced. He walked to the middle of the classroom. He did not have to ask me to follow. I followed slowly. All eyes on me.

He told me to put my hands out. I lifted my right hand with the palm open, halfway towards him. He reached down and grabbed my black hand and pulled it towards him. Palms open. He held my hand with my middle finger, raised the whip. The whip whooshed in the air as he raised it. Eyes closed tight; tears dry. It came slicing down onto my open palms. The crack sent a thunder across the school. Every eye looked towards the sound. Dead silence. I pulled away and screamed. The whip came cracking down on my ass as I screamed again. He pulled my hand as I made a fist again and cracked the whip across my knuckles. My hand opened, and he cracked the whip across my open palms. I cried. The more I cried, the more I got. Three seconds and another sliced the air, cutting into my hands. He stopped when I stopped crying, and he walked away towards his office. I stood there for a minute. Eyes on their desk as I walked back to my class and took my seat in the middle of the row. No one said a word to me. I stayed silent. The bell rang, and we all rose slowly and marched out of the school.

I sat with the pain. I tried to keep still, and the pain grew in my ass. My hands were red. I slowly opened them and prayed for the pain to leave. I gently blew on them, but the pain grew even greater. I cried. The pain would be there tomorrow and the day after until I got the answer wrong again.

Lix for dirty shoes, unbleached white shoes, dirty fingernails, wrinkled uniform, chewing gum, late, wrong answers, lowest marks, talking in class, no book covers, no numbered pages, greasy hair, didn't say Sir, didn't say Miss, dirty white pages.

Mustn't dirty the master's books. Whose books? Your books? No, the master's books.

This is Jane,
This is Dick,
See Jane skip,
See Dick run.

After school we ran towards the open savannah. We threw our books on the ground. We did not care; it was time for three-hole marbles. We just wanted to win all the marbles, especially the coloured marbles; KK marbles were flawless. They were winning marbles. When you were good at marbles, you had to be prepared to fight for them. Holding the marble between your fingers, you concentrated and took aim. The marble flew and shot and exploded your opponent's marbles. There was a thunder of applause.

The winner did not get away that easy. You would need your older brother or the biggest bully to take you home. When playing marbles, the poor kids must lose. The rich kids must win. The fair skin kids must win. Those were the unwritten rules. Kids did cry when they lost. Then parents got involved. That meant giving back what you won.

KK marbles are like an HB pencil that was Hard Blackness. Made in England. Mame called the pencil "Hard Body." When you are holding a HB pencil between your fingers, the answer is always right. We learned never to substitute the best; you just did not do it, and it was simply never done. You could tell who was poor and who was rich by their pencils. The poor wrote with charcoal, and the rich wrote with HB pencils.

An HB pencil was long, wooden, and majestic. Six-sided hexagons. The outside painted yellow. Sharp black lead in the middle of the shaft, covered by a light-brown wood. You held your pencil firmly between your thumb and index finger.

We were inspected daily for sharp pencils and unused erasers. Used erasers meant wrong answers, and this was a sign that you were a dunce and it was time for lix. The paper was white and bleached, and you had to number the upper right-hand corners. You had to write straight, with no crooked lines. At the top of the pencil was a gold metal casing holding the pink eraser, which you were not allowed to use.

You had to think hard before taking pencil to paper. Making a mistake caused you to erase. Erasing stains, smearing the paper with blackness. You must never trespass on the margin. Words were carefully watched on bleached paper.

Mrs. Hatchet paced the centre of the classroom. She stopped beside you and said, "Bring your books to me."

There was no name, but you knew it was you. You took your time collecting your books, knowing you must hurry, knowing she was impatient with you. She counted the seconds. She knew there were pages missing and pages stained with black marks across them. There were scribbles of wrong answers to questions you did not understand. Answers that you copied from someone else.

As you approached the desk, she pulled out the whip from the draw, the whip you had picked earlier in the day. The tears welled up in your eyes as you walked to the front of the class without your books. You extended your hand, eyes shut tightly. You kept your right hand steady as the whip came down.

Today you got two across the palm of your hands. You walked slowly back to the desk and sat down quietly. You waited patiently for the recess bell.

THE ABATTOIR

Two little piggies went to market.
Two little piggies never came home.
The abattoir was located just behind the house in
the savannah.

I hated the abattoir. Every morning I had to clean the
pig pens. Feed the hogs. Shovel the shit and wash the hogs
down. They must always be clean before going to the table.
The hate was small, then it grew into bigger hate. The smell
was twenty-four hours. The smell would not leave your nose.

Sometimes I felt the pigs understood me. They understood why they were here. The holding pens were dark. They
saw no sunlight until it was time for the table. Satisfaction
came only from death. The pigs were bad things, they were
evil. I would throw the slop in the well, and they would
waddle over to the trough and eat the garbage. Their food
was left over from the kitchen. Every night I would go
around the neighbourhood and collect the waste food and
bring it back to the abattoir. The scraps of food would be a
mixture of rice, chicken, and vegetables. Sometimes it was

hard to stomach the smell. They always knew when it was feeding time. There were loud squeals coming from the pen.

The pigs were large and heavy. Their stomachs dragged on the ground. They were fattened from the time they were born. They were pink and ugly. The fatter, the better.

While the goats, cows, chickens, and ducks ran free, the pigs and hogs were locked in the abattoir. Once in a while we would hear a grunt coming from inside.

Every Saturday morning, we would all gather on the wall of the abattoir to see the killing, the slaughter. The truck pulled up to the wooden gates as we all watched the men herd the pigs into the holding pen. The men were tall, with strong arms, big smiles, big laughter that came from the stomach. Hard-working men. Cane field during the week, then the abattoir on Saturdays.

We heard grunting and squealing from the truck as the pigs were tossed from side to side. All we could see as the truck passed by was eyes. Big eyes staring out at us.

The abattoir was a menacing grey and burgundy, with its own water tower. The smell was pig shit and pig shit. The interior was dried blood and pig hair in every corner. Depending on the wind direction, the smell went for miles. The interior was grey and cement-coloured. The main slaughter room was in the front of the building just as you entered. The furnace was not far from the slaughter table. It was the only fire going during the slaughtering.

The slaughter table was black. The table was long. The table sat still. It was solid mango wood. Well oiled and pre-served. The table sat in a dark room until Saturday morning.

It was quite heavy. It took four men to move the table into the slaughterhouse.

Uncle Selwyn was pitch black. He was dogla. His smile was pearl white. He had a gold tooth for one of his canines. He had two sons, just as black. His boys were outcast. They did not play cricket with us in the savannah. They spent most of their free time playing the steelpan. They were nicknamed Pork Lips, pig eaters by the rest of the boys.

The village was small. The majority were Indians, Muslims, and Africans. Most of the land was owned by the Indian and Muslim labourers, including the grocery shop and the Snack - it shop. The Indians were called Coolies and the Africans were Creoles, niggers, and dogla. Dogla were a mixed race of Indian and African. The village was rich, with two-storey concrete houses with a lot of land. The Africans were the poorest in the village. The Indian community was rich, with a backwards culture of arranged marriages. The dogla were cast out.

As the men herded the pigs into the abattoir, you heard the squealing and grunting from the pigs and hogs. Uncle Selwyn walked out of the building and looked over the herd, and he picked the ones for the front pen. He put the hogs in the back pen. The hogs were all black with hints of grey hair. As they were all herded into the abattoir, the men drank coffee from the fire. The coffee was pitch black and strong.

There was nothing cute about the pigs. We had no feeling for them. They were not more than three to six months old. Their squealing was loud and pained. In the first pen was a crowd of five pigs. I stared, and their eyes stared back. I had no feeling for the pigs. You could hear the fright. They were crowded in the pen and could not calm down.

One of the workers would lash out across the top of their heads to lead them into the abattoir. Some of the piglets showed excited resistance against the whip. The butcher cracked the whip again and they moved. The butcher cracked the whip again. They all slowly moved into the abattoir.

After they got all the pigs and hogs into the abattoir, we all scrambled from the outside fence to get a good position on the abattoir wall. The smaller kids with us had to stand near the doorway to get a look into the slaughter room. Most of the time we told them to get lost. We were the big kids and the cool kids. If a pig went and tried to escape death, you would have to scramble for your life and the older kids would have no time to protect the smaller kids. It was a dangerous place to be, on the floor. Every runt learned that lesson the first time at the abattoir. It was their initiation before they got a position on the wall.

From the top of the wall we could see the slaughter table, the furnace, and the giant hooks from the rafters that were used to hang the fresh meat for market. On the far wall there were buckets filled with rainwater to wash the pigs. Several steel buckets lined a bench to hold all the precious pig guts and blood.

We would hear the squealing and grunting from the pen and the sound of the cracking whip. The knives and the cutlass would be laid out on a table waiting for inspection. Everyone had their favourite knife. They would test the blade with their thumbs. They would smile with gleaming white teeth when they were pleased with the sharpness.

The smell of pig shit was everywhere. The smell was so heavy you could taste it. The hogs they brought in were overly fat and clumsy. The squealing and screaming would get louder as they were herded into the inner pens. The pens were small and compact, built to hold two to three hogs, depending on the size, but that didn't matter—up to six or seven pigs were forced into one pen.

As the butchers came into the abattoir, there was a "good morning" and a round of handshakes and questions about family. They were the same questions asked the week before, at the last slaughter, but it was a renewed ritual that brought happiness and soul. Everyone was pitch black. As one of the butchers passed the hot coffee from the edge of the fire, they would make sure each enamel cup was full of the dark, sweet-tasting gold. There would be joking and laughing, loud, hefty laughing, as more coffee and cane sugar was passed around. There was condensed milk as well, but it was refused without even a glance and the laughter would continue as they chided each other. After an hour of talking, laughing, and second cups of black coffee, it was time to start the first slaughter.

This Saturday there were five butchers in all. More animals were slaughtered at the end of the month and depending on the holidays. One of the butchers, a tall, pitch-black man with arms of steel and beautiful gleaming teeth, called for the first pig. Another butcher checked the ropes for weakness. The hooks, hanging from the rafters, were also checked for their strengths. Another one checked the gates. He would shout at the children, "Gawn": stand behind the iron gates. The furnace was checked for the blaze of fire, and the knives and cutlass were looked over one last time. Everyone had their favourites.

From the back of the pen we heard loud squealing as one of the hogs was dragged in with a noose around its neck. The hog was being stubborn, showing a lot of resistance, but the crack of the whip edged the hog closer to the table. The butcher stopped pulling the hog as he neared the table. Two other butchers came to assist him with the hog-tying. This hog was around two hundred pounds. It needed all three of them to tie it to the table. These men were called the lifters.

The hog sensed the danger and bolted for the gate. The kids scrambled to safety even though the gate was locked. The hog lunged at it, trying to escape, but the three butchers were fast. The hog was grabbed, with all the weight of the three men on it. It was hog-tied and easily lifted and thrown on the table. Once on the table, the hog was held down and tied again. The hog was squealing an ear-piercing sound. We covered our ears and looked in fright. The hog squealed wildly with its head hanging over the edge of the table. The strength of the hog moved the table, and the butchers held the hog down and gently massaged it with easy strokes.

The loud squealing of the other pigs from the back of the abattoir accompanied the squealing hog on the table. There was a deafening symphony of chorus in the building that could be heard across the savannah. In the distance, people looked up in the direction the sound was coming from.

We all covered our ears as the deafening symphony of death continued, and the worker in the back cracked the whip for silence, but the squealing did not stop.

The hog, tied to the table, reached a calm as the three butchers gently massaged the beast. There were just low grunts. They moved the table back to the centre of the room. The squealing pigs in the back pen stopped.

Uncle Selwyn got his knife ready and called for the blood bucket to be put at the edge of the table, just below the over-hanging head. The bucket was in place and a bucket of rainwater was ready. The hog was quiet. The back pen was dead silence. We all stared from the wall. Everyone waited with anticipation for Uncle Selwyn to begin.

The knife was his way to end life, to take what was not his. It was his to take what he could not create—this fat, overstuffed hog with waving fat—precious blood pudding.

Uncle Selwyn called for the Wilkinson blades, shaving cream, and hot water from the edge of the fire, to shave the hog's neck. A lather of shaving cream was pasted onto the neck, and slowly, Uncle Selwyn shaved the hog's neck as he would his own. Uncle Selwyn usually allowed one of the new butchers to do this, but today he felt different and wanted to do it himself.

First, the hot water opened the pores of the skin and softened it. Then he lathered the cream onto the neck. The blade was dipped in hot water. He brought the blade to the skin and took firm strokes upwards, dragging the hair out. He dipped the blade in the hot water after each stroke.

As he stroked the hog, his mind saw his face in the mirror. As the strokes continued, he saw his smooth, masculine jawline; he was manly. High cheekbones, ebony skin. He thought of a Greek statue as he stared at himself in the mirror. He was pleased and silently kissed the mirror and saw how beautiful he was. Uncle Selwyn woke up from his trance and slapped the neck of the hog. The hog jumped. The hair fell loosely to the ground, and he passed the blade to his skinner.

During this time, the hog was incredibly quiet. The hog was relaxed on the table. It had gotten used to being tied and bound securely with the three men massaging him. The hog was calm. From the back pen we heard very few squeals.

From the top of the walls we watched with attention. We could see and hear every move on the floor. As the hog scrambled for his life and lurched off the table. We all screamed for the butchers to catch it. We screamed and laughed as the hog tried to get away. There was no escape for the hog; the gates and the doors were locked tight, but the hog could move fast. He was fat and clumsy, but a madness overtook the hog as he tried to escape from the abattoir.

This unseen strength to escape—where did it come from? The hog squealed a piercing squeal, biting and lunging at the butchers, trying to escape into the open savannah air. We all watched with wide-open eyes as the hog was caught, bound by the hooves, and thrown onto the slaughter table. The table sat silently waiting.

Uncle Selwyn finished shaving the hog. The other three butchers continued to rest their weight on top of the hog. They gently stroked and massaged the hog. It quieted down. Uncle Selwyn reached for the cutting knife and tested the edge once again with his thumb. He looked at the bucket at the edge of the table making sure it was directly under the head to collect the blood.

With a blank look on his face, Uncle Selwyn sliced into the pink flesh. A loud squeal came out of the hog as Uncle Selwyn dug deep into the hog's throat. The butchers held the head down and placed more pressure on the table to stop the hog from moving. The blood spurted and then splashed across the hands of Uncle Selwyn. The hog shook the table as life left his body. The hog twisted its head violently, trying to break the grip of the knife in its throat. It was a simple cut, but deep. The table moved across the room. The hog had great strength.

They tightened the hold on the hog's head. The blood started spurting everywhere. They had to hold the head firmly over the bucket. Uncle Selwyn pulled the knife out and the hog's head fell limp. He passed the knife over to be cleaned and sharpened again. The blood burst out of the hog like a dam. The blood started to pool in the bucket, filling it fast. They had to rush and get another bucket. As the thick blood filled the bucket, the oxygen bubbles burst and escaped in the air. The hog laid limp.

With his hands drenched in blood, Uncle Selwyn called for water. He watched as the last ounce of life drifted out of the hog. With the buckets filled, the butchers relaxed and pushed the table back to the middle of the room. Their white uniforms were soaked in red. They relaxed the ropes on the hog and proceeded to remove them.

The squealing was loud and sharp. Ear-splitting. Loud, chilling squeals. Sad screams to say goodbye to the first on the table. The master cracked the whip to keep the pen quiet. As much as he tried, the cries would not stop. The pigs were mourning.

From the top of the wall we watched in silence. As Uncle Selwyn took the knife, the smaller kids had shut their eyes. Some of them ran away. The hog was untied from the table and hoisted to the rafters. The dogla butcher lowered the hooks from the upper beams. The chain came down. The hooks pierced the hooves of the hogs and hoisted to the rafters. With the hog hanging in the air, he called for the gutter. This was the easy part. After the killing, Uncle Selwyn usually stayed silent for three to five minutes.

The gutter was responsible for cutting open the belly and collecting all the intestines. They were quite heavy and needed a good knife operator. A clean white bucket was placed under the hog to collect the last remaining blood. The eyes were now squinting, and life had left the body. With the hog hanging from its back hooves, we noticed the clean cut. Uncle Selwyn was enormously proud of his work. The animal did not suffer.

The bucket was now replaced with a large plastic tub. Uncle Selwyn went to wash the blood off his hands, which was starting to dry. The gutter took long strides to the hog with cutlass in hand. The hog hung with its guts falling inside its belly towards its head. Uncle Selwyn examined his work again with pleasure. A stool was placed just underneath the hog. Uncle Selwyn stepped up to the hog and took yellow chalk out of his apron and drew a line on the centre of the hog's belly, from the bottom of the tail to the lower lip. He put the chalk back into his apron pocket. The gutter waited patiently until Uncle Selwyn stepped back.

The gutter made a shallow cut on the line Uncle Selwyn drew, being very careful. With the hog's belly bulging, he cut deeper until he split the underbelly open. The guts came pouring out and landed in the tub. Close to fifty pounds of guts came pouring out. The heart and liver were left attached. Uncle Selwyn walked up to the hog and sliced a piece of the liver off with a paring knife he kept in his pocket. He tossed it into the fire. After a couple of minutes, he reached in and stabbed it with the knife. He blew on the piece of liver and popped it into his mouth.

After the gutter was finished, he called for the splitter, who was a strong, muscular man. Two more butchers would hold the hog while he split the animal in half. With the legs spread from the rafters, he stepped up and brought the cutlass down onto the hog, splitting it in half. This took longer than expected because of the spine he had to split. With all his strength, he brought down each blow with full force. He split the hog in half and the other two butchers caught it as it split. The hog was pushed to the end of the rafters. Uncle Selwyn was happy with the kill.

We hear the pigs squealing from the back of the pen. The squealing was getting loud. The table was washed down and ready again.

To market, to market to buy a fat pig,
home again, home again, jiggety-jig
To market, to market to buy a fat hog
home again, home again, jiggety-jog

LIVE

Live Evil
For Evil is Live.
And the Devil has Lived.

WHEN BLACK MEN KISS

Two little dickie birds
Sat on a wall
One named Peter
One named Paul
Fly away, Peter, fly away, Paul
Come back, Peter, come back, Paul

His skin was sweet as honey. His face soft and smooth. An angel looks in his eyes. His eyes were warm, inviting, and caressing. I remember his skin pressing against mine as he held me tight. And his eyes were a deep ocean of blue.

I can still see myself in his crystal-blue eyes.

The smile, the smile was warm, inviting, and safe. His arms, oh, his arms would hold me tight. I felt warm and safe. Holding me tightly, he pressed hard, gentle kisses against my face. He pressed his mouth into my belly and blew back and forth. I laughed and laughed as he tickled me. He held me tight as I wiggled frantically in his arms. He was kissing my belly, my soft belly, my neck, gently biting my me. With sweet, gentle bites.

Today I want to be bitten, bitten very hard as my memory flows back to those days.

I am laughing louder and louder. He is throwing me up in the air and I am trusting him, every moment giving myself to him knowing I will fall safely in his arms, never fearing, never losing his love, his trust. He spins me in circles as I pretend to be an airplane; he is making the sound of the plane flying across the sky that is blue like his eyes.

He hangs me upside down and swings me over the banister. I am laughing and laughing as he swings me over the railing. Then he picks me up, throws me up in the air, and I turn in mid-air, arms stretched out towards him, and he catches me, hugs me tightly, and I return the warm embrace and kiss his face as he lets me down to run and play on my own. I wanted that warm hug to hold me tightly forever.

When he left, I would cry until I fell asleep. His was the last face I saw before I drifted off into tiredness. I wanted to run away with him. As I drifted into sleep, he snuck out the door. Morning came and I was looking all over the house for him.

"Where is he?" I was screaming

"He'll be back soon," Mame answered.

Then I saw him less and less until I saw him no more.

As black as pitch, as black as tar, with ivory teeth. I knew who I was. The neighbours were talking, and my aunts and uncles were talking. Then all the kids were calling me. I just knew the name. It stayed in my head; from the playground to the walk home, I would think, "Battyboy, Battyman" . . . the sound was loud and deafening, like clapping thunder and lightning slashing across the savannah.

"Boy, stay out of the cane field; you want the Battyman to get ya?"

The night was heavy with rain. Thunder rolling across the savannah. The wind pelting the rain in no direction. I was screaming and kicking.

From the day I was born, my blackness enveloped me. My skin was flawless. My skin was black as night. My thoughts were black. My body black. My lips black. I voted black. I caused political turmoil with my blackness. Faces shocked, gasping sounds as I came into the world. I was blacker than the pitch outside during the noon sun. My body shone and glistened as Mame oiled my body in coconut oil.

At six I told no one my thoughts and dreams or the things I saw when I closed my eyes and looked into the distance. They were my thoughts, my secrets that I stored inside of me. Hidden in all my blackness. Mame would sit and talk to me for hours on end, and still I would not tell. There was no one, no father and no Nana. Mame and me tried to look after each other. The closest relationship, a closeness not even my first love and I would share. Blunt and hurting closeness.

When I was six years old, we played on the beach, running and skipping on the Caribbean sand. We played catch the waves. We collected all the seashells we could carry in our little hands. I stared into the sea. I was afraid. I did not go into the sea. I played with her. We had a game of "catch me if you can." I would chase her as she receded, and she would roll towards me with white, foaming waves. Like a herd of prancing horses. She was fast, and I was faster. The deep blue Caribbean Sea. She didn't like me even though we played the game. She was big, and the horizon was far and wide. There was no end to the sky. I was afraid, always afraid. At night I woke up to drowning. She was covering me and I was frantically fighting to escape her. I was ripping into her, tearing her apart, but she held me tight.

So, I stayed at the water's edge as she came in night after night. Each wave the sound of my name, calling me to taste her salty lips. I was afraid of that feeling of stifling. The water rushing, wave after wave covering me. Her arms holding me tight as I frantically fought. I was screaming for her to let me go. Night after night the nightmares came as white-water swirled around me. Pulling me into a blinding whiteness. I was screaming out with lashing arms, with no sign of opening. My arms limp and tired from the fighting. I was worn out, too tired to move as my arms fall lifeless and clung to my sides. I passed out.

I stayed on the beach playing with the sea. Running towards her waves as she pulled herself away from the land. I ran after her and ran back as she was coming towards me. I ran faster than her.

"Catch me if you can."

I would watch the fishermen come in with the catch and help them unload the catch. "Hey, may you return" and the catch be bountiful. Times were getting rough, with less fish, and farther out into the sea they would have to go, some not returning for days and long nights. The women prayed every morning that they may return safely, and the catch may be bountiful. Times were getting hard with less fish in the sea. Families would show up every night on the jetty, looking across the open sea for any sign of the incoming boats.

The beach was bronze and gold from the hot sun beating down on the surface for miles and miles. In the sunlight, the sand glistened with millions and millions of tiny diamonds. With each crashing wave, the sand would build higher and higher on the banks. I continued to run to the edge of the sea and run back before the waves would catch me. At six years old I was afraid, and I was trying to beat her. At six years old I was having fun on the beach.

The sun was setting in the Caribbean Sea of brilliant blue. Going somewhere else to see the world, and the moon was rising across the horizon to say hello. The sea was waves of fiery orange as the sun set. The sun setting was my only evidence that God existed. This was God. The light on the waves and the colour of the fiery reds and orange. The magic of God. Looking for hope in the distance, he came in waves.

"I am here and will always be here for you." "I am inside of you."

The sun blazed across the horizon as she stretched her arms out, reaching to the ends of the earth. The tide was rising, and we had to stay closer to the shore where we all could be seen by the last light. We all stared in awe as the sun continued to reach across the universe. The colour of God stretched and reached inside of me. Our eyes closed as the light bathed us in colour, in warmth, as waves crashed and pounded the earth. The moon was pulling and slapping the rocks on the beach, and the sea washing the mangrove clean of all the jumbie crabs clinging to the mangrove trees. The rocks became smooth as each slap of the wave moved in harder and harder. The seagulls and the pelicans quieted for the night. The sky was turning in a movement of blackness. In the distance, the sky blackened with a wave of bats.

The fishing boats were all coming in for the night with the catch of the day. The boats were old and beaten up from all the storms and hurricanes they had been through. This season was very rough for hurricanes. A lot of fishermen lost their boats from the last storm. They made a lot of noise pulling up to the jetty. Engines were puttering. Everyone was looking to see that they would all make it to the jetty in one piece. The engines' puttering was getting worse as they pulled up to the jetty. The sound got worse as they were anchored. The smokestacks were puffing and belching out black, thick smoke.

The boats were all in a state of disarray; some would not make it next season. The catch must be bountiful this season if any repairs were to happen. The boats were all colourful, with white, blue, red, and orange stripes. Some were solid green with white trim. Paint was peeling from the hard-working boats. No one paid much attention to this ugliness so long as the boats didn't sink and could bring the catch in and the family could come back home at night.

There were tugboats and long rowboats. The long boats could carry up to eight men at a time. The head of the chanter sang to the rowers to keep rowing. They kept in rhythm with his song. The song was sad. The catch was little. This meant the little would have to be shared with the rest of the boats and families. Tomorrow would be better.

There was always tomorrow. They would pray the ocean would be full. They would pray God would give favour.

The jetty was filling with families coming to greet husbands and sons from the ocean. The flambeau was being lit along the jetty to light the night and ward off the hungry mosquitoes from the mangroves. As the boats pulled in, the oil can fire were already cooking the fresh catch of the day.

Big iron pots were being placed on the fires as they blazed. The sun continued to set in the distance. The flambeau added their colour to the setting sun. As the engine boats pulled in along the beach, we could see spots of lights coming on in the darkness of the mangroves. Darkness here was pitch black.

The huts and shacks were made of scraps of wood, coconut branches, and galvanized steel found on the beach. They were built just leaning up against each other, with bricks on the roof to hold them down. The rain on the galvanized roof was a sweet sound at night. Strong winds from the sea would blow the houses down. No one would complain, and no one would form a committee. They were squatters. The squatters' homes were close to the burning bag gas. Bag gas was dry husk from cane shoots after the juice was extracted. The cane factory used the mangrove to burn the shoots. The cane fire burned all day and night. The fire kept the area warm at night.

The music started as the boats pulled in closer to the jetty to unload the fish. A young black boy as black as pitch, with ebony glistening skin, started beating an oil can hanging around his neck with two rubber tips. The women walked and swayed their hips to the rhythm of his beat. The young black boy was not more than eleven. He knew every note on the pan like the back of his black tar hand. With the draw of the music, the jetty was getting crowded with people, laughter, and the sweet aroma of fresh-cooked fish.

The Caribbean sunset, a feeling of love of seeing for the first time. God was rising and God was setting but never sleeping. As the sun was set, the moon rose higher in the sky, bringing the waves, leaving layers of sand on the beach, covering all God's footsteps with each wave that came in. Each wave destroying the sandcastles from the daylight. Waves crashing and slamming in the distance. The moon pulling each wave as she rose in the sky, the sun running in the distance. As the sun set, the waves carried the last lights to the shore; as it hit, it disappeared into the sand. The light buried itself beneath the layers of sand that even destroyed God's footsteps. The game between the sun and the moon and the sea continued, with the sun losing night after night as she dipped into the ocean at the far end of the world.

The music reached a higher pitch as the dance on the jetty continued, with the moon bathing the worshippers of the night sea. The tides rose higher and higher, slapping the rocks in the distance, adding their own hypnotic beat to the steelpan. The crashing of the incoming waves and the beating of the steelpan were accompanied by the women singing "Thank you, oh Lord, the sea is mine." They sang in chorus as the men came off the boats. We stared in amazement at the magic of the setting sun sinking in the distance, the golden rays spreading the arms of God across the sea, the moon and the ocean controlling the shadows, forcing them to move and sway uncontrollably to heights of magic from the moon and the sun as the sea beat the land.

The sun finally gave the sea its last ray of light and vanished for the night, losing, as always, night after night. Leaving the moon and the sea and the music of the pan to play the rest of the night away. Limbs and hips moved through the night, forming hypnotic shadows on the jetty. The fresh fish cooking, the wind sending its aroma of fish stew, grilled shark on the open oil can. The bottles of rum and puncheon and sweet coconut water passed from hand to hand, shadow to shadow. The young boy continued to play the steelpan as hot food was passed around and everyone ate until full.

I played in the sand as the sea ate the sun and the moon rose higher in the sky. My brothers and sisters huddled closer to Mame when the music started, and everyone arrived on the jetty for the cook-up. There was a look of fright on their faces as the sun set. They were screaming for the sun not to go away. As the sun dipped on the horizon, the moon rose higher, pulling heavier waves with her. The laughter on the jetty was getting louder as more shadows filled the jetty. The shadows were getting louder and louder, drowning out the waves being pulled by the sun crashing and slamming on the beach.

The sunlight disappeared on the horizon, the children screaming for her to stay. The moon was now casting her light over the shadows on the jetty, the silhouette of the shadows bathing flying arms and bodies moving to the rhythm of the steelpan. They were frightened and could not take their eyes off the shadows on the jetty.

Mame stared at the jetty and called for calm as they clung to her sari like frightened sheep about to be slaughtered. Mame moved my brothers and sisters farther up the beach, away from the music and the shadows on the jetty. The tugboats sounded their horns to the rhythm of the steelpan. The sound was loud and frightening. The children screamed to go home. The beach was becoming very frightening.

"Let's go home," they screamed.

"Mame, hurry, they will get us."

"Don't be silly, now stop being stupid. We are leaving," she answered.

They fought the music. The music tried to enter their souls. To enter their bodies. They fought the steelpan. They fought the boy with his spellbinding music. They fought the moon, the sea, and the shadows on the jetty. Angry with the setting sun, they screamed for home.

Inviting waves, they called to come and join the fete on the jetty. I waved in answer. I jumped in the air, I twisted my body and moved my hips to the spell, the spell cast by the pan boy on the jetty. Everyone ate their fill and settled down to talk of old jumbie stories and stories of the big one that got away and how they hoped the season was profitable. Laughter mounted as the stories reached a climax of funny exaggerations. The steelpan continued to play to a slow, hypnotic rhythm. The shadows mellowed down to rest, their bellies full.

The night stood still. The sun long gone, now off in the horizon, having lost the battle with the moon. The moon continued to climb in the sky, casting an eerie light across the jetty. The shadows showed eyes piercing into the pitch-black night. Gentle waves crashed in the distance as the moonlight reached farther into the mangroves. The squatters' lights were going out along the beach, their galvanized roofs lit by the moon and the stars coming out in the sky.

STATION 1

Jesus is condemned to death.

The pitch blackness of night. The cracking of thunder. The smoke rising from the burning cane. Thunderous screaming coming from the mangrove awoke the jetty in a fright. The steelpan came to a full stop as the shadows rose from their slumber of the cook-up with ears pointing towards the mangrove. The waves froze in mid-air. The stars died. The lights along the beach died. The laughter, the steelpan, the storyteller, the hum of the boats, came to a dead stop. Crashing waves were silenced. The beating and slapping of the rocks died. In the pitch darkness of the mangrove, the scream grew louder as the lights from the squatters' huts died.

STATION 2

Jesus accepts the cross.

All eyes on the jetty turned towards the sound coming out of the mangroves. In the pitch darkness, the scream grew louder. The wailing rose higher and higher. Whips were cracking in the darkness. The sound of an animal roaring in pain. The scream came closer and closer, out of the darkness towards the jetty. Slowly, the shadows rose, the sound of the whip cutting into the darkness.

STATION 3

Jesus falls for the first time under his cross.

Lashes landed on bare backs, piercing flesh into redness as the animal screamed for mercy. The flambeau and the oil cans were fired on the jetty as shadows rose to light the night to see the animal coming out of the blackness. The screaming penetrated the heads of the shadows. They had heard this scream before. The wailing, the call for mercy. The shadows stared into the pitch of night. Waiting to see what was coming.

STATION 4

Jesus meets his sorrowful mother.

Eyes opened wide as the master cracked his whip to move Blackness into the bowels of the ship. They stumbled forward into the belly of the ship. Not knowing where they were going. Never to see their continent again. They followed the shackled line as they slowly piled into the bowels of the ship. Whips cracking on their backs.

Eyes stared and waited to see the sound coming out of the darkness. The moon, high above the mangrove, bathed the scream in light. The red came pouring out of the Blackness as the figure stumbled forward. Hands covering the face, the blows fell and struck with no mercy. From the jetty, the shadows rose in sequence and ran towards the fallen animal. A woman reached the fallen animal and looked down to eyes staring back at her.

Redness falling, pouring out of Blackness; the figure tried to break free. The eyes stared back at her and silently begged for mercy.

"Mame," she heard in the darkness.

It was no animal, but it was on all fours.

Then she heard a voice behind her: "Battyman."

She stared in shock. She grabbed a stick and started to beat him.

STATION 5
Simon of Cyrene helps Jesus to carry his cross.

He begged for mercy, but he just received staring eyes. The whips came crashing down on his back. The shadows surrounded the man as he tried to get up. The wailing was deafening. He screamed for mercy. He screamed, "God." The whites of his eyes were covered in blood. His hands in prayer, he continued to beg for mercy.

"Stop, please stop," he begged.

The pan boy stared in fright as he saw whip after whip crash down on him. The pan boy reached down to help him up. A whip came crashing down on the boy's back as he was pulled away from him.

"Mercy," he screamed.

"Oh, God of Mercy," he cried.

STATION 6
Veronica wipes the face of Jesus.

A black woman stepped in the way of the whip as it came crashing down on his back. She took her scarf and wiped his face. She stared as she saw his eyes staring back at her.

"Mame," he whispered.

STATION 7
Jesus falls for the second time.

The beating stopped. She picked him up and tried to carry him. She could not carry him. Blood flowed from him like a river. She was soaked in red. The whip pierced the pitch-black skin. Cutting into his flesh, exposing whiteness and instantly flowing red. Red flowed thick out of darkness into the night salt air. He had fallen again, grabbing the ground. The wailing for mercy. Mercy to end it all.

STATION 8
The women of Jerusalem weep over Jesus.

The shadow of women wept. No one knew why this was happening. The crowd was hell. This was hell. As eyes waited to see the sound coming out of the darkness. He continued to stumble; he was prodded with an iron poker to get up. The moonlight cast a light over the mangroves. The shadows on the jetty rose and ran towards the light. The darkness poured more red. The women screamed when they saw the man on the ground.

STATION 9
Jesus falls for the third time.

My eyes saw the pain. I could not turn away. In the back of my head, I heard Mame calling me. The shadows screamed to beat him more. More whips and chains. Cries to kill him. The lashes fell like thunder in the darkness. With each fall, he was prodded to get up. Children poked him with long sticks. Screaming for him to get up. He crawled to try and get away, but there was nowhere to go. The gravel on the ground pierced his wounds even further. As he fell, they poked at him to get up.

STATION 10
Jesus is stripped of His garments.

As he slowly crawled to the beach, they grabbed his torn clothes and ripped them off his back. Soaked in blood, they continue to prod him on.

He cried with praying hands for God as the lashes bore down on him.

"God help me, oh God, help me."

"Please stop," he cried.

STATION 11
Jesus is nailed to the cross.

He cried and he cried to silence and still he cried to God.

"Father, help me, oh God, help me."

He begged them to stop. "Oh God, help me," he cried.

As he cried and begged for mercy, the lashes fell to deaf ears. They pulled and poked at him with bamboo sticks to get up and move. The shadows grew larger and larger around the bloodied figure as he was dragged closer to the sea. He reached out with hands to pray and beg forgiveness. With weak hands, he continued to shield his face to stop the blows to his head. The blood poured out of his ribs, out of his legs. Out of his back. Flowed out of his face. Out of his mouth.

With hands in pray he cries Mama, help me.

STATION 12

Jesus dies on the cross.

The sea waited silently with open arms. The sun long gone. No longer here to cast her beams on incoming waves. The sea sent gentle waves. The shadows gathered around the fallen man and lifted him to the salty air and threw him into the arms of the sea.

The moon moved across the sky, silently staring, casting her light on the ceremony. The sea took her gift. She drew back from the man, then came in to swallow the ebony man. The open wounds received the burning salt as he screamed to whip the sea apart. He screamed a cry from hell. He screamed for death to come quickly. The distant stars blinked.

The moon high above bathed the sea with rays. The distant stars blinked quietly. The sea covered him, not letting him go as he frantically fought her with flaring arms. Each incoming wave grew higher and higher as she drew him into her bosom. She cleansed his soul. With wild, flaring arms, he tried to break free. She held him, not letting go. His lungs filled with water. His wounds burnt with salt. The shadows walked away. Everyone slowly headed back to the jetty. The pan boy, crying, started a slow beat.

"Come on, come on, we must go," I heard in the back of my head.

STATION 13

Jesus is taken down from the cross.

I stood staring at the sea. The sea, no longer wanting him, threw him onto the beach. The moon no longer bathed the shadows in her light as she climbed higher in the night sky. He lay motionless. A black shadow. The sound of seagulls flying in the distance. The waves stopped pushing him onto the beach. He lay motionless. The moon left the sky. Passing clouds covered her face. She did not want to see what the sea had spat out.

STATION 14

Jesus is laid in the sepulchre.

"Come on, come on, we must go," rang in my ears, drawing me back from the shadows. The shadow lay motionless on the sand with billions of tiny diamonds that glistened in the sunlight. The waves moved in and out, the wounds washed clean.

At the end, the sea of life does not accept the Battyman's body; she refuses to kill him, to take responsibility for the act of murder.

Michael, row the boat ashore, hallelujah
Michael, row the boat ashore.

IT IS NOT A POODLE

I had been in Vancouver for three days. The day I went looking for an apartment I was staying with two friends in Coquitlam. They warned me that it was going to be expensive. That is what they said: expensive. I was there barely three days and found a place in the West End of Vancouver, on Burnaby Street. Barely an hour after signing the application, I got a call saying the apartment was mine.

I have always been lucky. When I set my mind to do something, I always win. Within two hours of looking, I got a one-bedroom, third-floor apartment with an entrance foyer, mail to the door, a living room, dining room, multiple closets, large windows facing the parking lot and dumpster in the alley, and a balcony, or occasional wading pool when it rains. If I leaned over without falling and looked between two buildings, I saw English Bay. To get to the beach, I had to leave the apartment.

On the first day I was on Burnaby Street, I was walking towards Denman and Davie streets. This was supposedly the Gay Village. I was still waiting to see it. There were lots of apartment buildings with "for rent" signs. The street was clean, with manicured lawns. As I walked, two queens sitting on their Romeo and Juliet balcony waved to me.

I waved back. I was young, they were not blind yet, I was hot. I sucked my stomach in. They were dilapidated but had great smiles and good Lord, one of 'em was wearing a straw floral hat. You know, the cheap straw hats from a Chinese store with the plastic flowers attached to them.

Just as I reached a corner, two black birds started squawking above me. I looked up and saw I was passing under their nest. The tree was a good two storeys high, and I could not reach their nest, so I was not worried about being attacked. But the squawking was loud. I ignored them. I passed it off as nature.

When I moved in, I explored the neighbourhood. I found the Starbucks on Davie. I walked up Denman. I found the pottery and the gym at the community centre. I shopped at Capers. Before, I had worked in Surrey at the Gilmore Mall. It was frightening. I was carded the second day I was there. I would not wish this on anyone. I was surrounded by two plainclothes officers. Then I eventually moved to Metropolis Mall in Burnaby, closer to my home.

Life in Vancouver was not lonely. It was just life. I got up, I went to work, I went to the gym, I shopped at Capers, I had coffee on Davie and Denman. I walked along English Bay, I saw the sunrise, I saw the sunset. All by myself.

Everyone that was gay had a boyfriend or were gay/straight married. Even looking at the ads online, you had to be available weekdays, mornings, afternoons. His place, your place. Into fucking, sucking, rimming, jerking off, ass play, nipple play, roleplay, three-way groups, water sports.

Seeking: open relationship, discreet, jocks, bodybuild-
ers, daddies, blue collar, Twinks, Chubbies, businessmen,
straight men, bi guys, younger, older, bears.

Turn ons: uniforms, suits, underwear, lingerie, sex toys,
porn, poppers, facials, cum eating, cum swapping.

Turn offs: Pain, scat, and blood, body odour,
poor hygiene.

Oh my God, I did not even know what some of these
things mean.

When I moved in, I got a pair of binoculars as a house-
warming present from my friends. Everyone laughed. I did
not, because I did not know what they were for, other than
bird watching.

I eventually learned why they gave me the binoculars.
My neighbours across the alley loved to have hetero living-
room window sex on the couch, with him on top. Right
after dinner.

I lost my job at the Gilmore Mall. I hated my boss, I
hated my co-workers, I hated cheap clothing, and I hated
getting up in the morning to take the SkyTrain from Burrard
Station. Since I had more time on my hands every morning,
I got dressed to cruise the neighbourhood. I sucked in my
stomach more often.

Across from my building lived a handsome George
Clooney lookalike with salt-and-pepper hair. He was very
handsome, but I had never seen him with anyone. The first
time I saw him he eyed me, and I ignored him. I can see if
someone is hot from a distance, but I do not have to let him
know I see him.

So, this cat and dog game went on a week. It was three days before I flew east. I woke up and breakfasted and felt like an outdoor patio on Davie, coffee with chocolates. I wore orange flip flops, yellow shorts above my knee, a green, short-sleeve striped shirt, and zirconia studs. That morning I had shaved my head and face, and I had cocoa-buttered skin from head to toe, deodorant, and Vaselined lips; on a hot day they look like pork lips. It was Ray Ban weather, so I had my aviators with the gold rims on and my Banana Republic duffle khaki sling bag on my left shoulder.

I elevatored down to the lobby, pushed the front doors open, and walked out to the sidewalk. I looked up and saw Mr. George Clooney Lookalike across the street. He had just walked out the door with a poodle who had a rainbow leash and collar.

I looked on, shocked. I was disgusted. I was, OMG, aghast. The poodle had just finish doing a poodle poop. The handsome George Clooney bent over with a plastic bag in his hand to pick up the poodle poop.

As I turned away, still in disgust, I started up the hill on Burnaby Street towards Jervis Street. The sun was shining, and a gentle breeze was moving pillow clouds across the blue sky. I could smell English Bay. I reached Jervis Street and I turned around and saw him looking at me. The poodle was sniffing the grass. I looked up the street and thought, "What the hell." I pushed my Ray Bans above my forehead, crossed the street, and walked straight towards him. I stopped in front of his patch of grass and I said, "Excuse me."

He looked at me with a sweet smile and the poodle looked up at me with exposed teeth. He said, "Yes" in an extremely hard French accent. I melted but still kept my composure.

I said, "I do not mind you walking your poodle on my street. I do not mind your poodle peeing on my grass. I do not care if you are picking your poodle's poop off the grass. But a poodle?" I pointed to the poodle, who was staring at me.

He stared at the poodle, he stared at me. The poodle stared at me.

In a heavy French accent that melted me, he said, "IT IS NOT A POODLE!"

I stared at him, aghast. *How dare you speak to me in that tone*, I thought.

The poodle stared at me; George Clooney stared at me. I stared at the poodle. It was a three-way stareathon. Who was going to win? We played this staring game for a few seconds, which seem like minutes. Suddenly the poodle growled with gaping teeth. His teeth were overlapping each other. It was a long, ten-second growl.

I turned on the spot. I grabbed my Ray Bans and started running up the hill. The poodle started barking and pulled his rainbow leash from George Clooney and started chasing me. I made it to Jervis Street when I heard George Clooney screaming after the poodle, "Fifi Fifi! Fifi!"

I was running, my flip flops flip-flopping up the hill, slapping my heels. As I hit Burnaby Street and Jervis Street, I made a dash for it. I heard a car coming, and I was going to make it across the street.

"Fifi! Fifi! Fifi!" George Clooney was running and screaming after his poodle.

As I dashed across the street, I heard the car coming to a screeching halt as Fife ran across the road, with George Clooney on his tail. George Clooney screamed.

My bag was beating my ass and back, and it dragged me down as I tried to outrun the poodle and George Clooney. My flip flops were pounding the pavement.

As I ran across the street in a mad dash, a swooping, squawking black bird came torpedoing towards my head. I screamed, "OMG!" I pulled my duffle bag off and held it over my head to stop the birds from attacking. I screamed at the birds with a clenched fist, "You idiots!"

Behind me, I heard the swooping black birds squawking and George Clooney still screaming and the poodle barking.

"Fifi! Fifi! Fifi!"

As I was running, the neighbours flocked to their balconies and yards to look at the confusion.

"You run, girl!" I heard the queens scream from their balcony.

I was flipping and flopping with my orange flip flops as they slapped my heels, with Fife close by. I was huffing and puffing as I ran with my Banana Republic duffle bag over my head. Just as I was about to hit Bute Street, my right flip flop got caught on a crack on the sidewalk and the thong ripped as the sole went flying behind me, still attached to my ankle. I let go of my duffle bag, and as it went flying, the strap choked me as I screamed. I hit the pavement with my outstretched palms and my knees scraped the pavement, bruising my right knee. I stayed down.

I could still hear "Fifi! Fifi!" as George Clooney caught his poodle. I lay on the sidewalk, pulling myself together.

My right knee had a sheet of blood on it. I stayed still until the queens showed up to help me.

Lesson learned: do not run in flip flops up a hill.

I ONLY MAKE LOVE IN MONTRÉAL

*"YOU HAVEN'T MADE LOVE UNTIL
YOU HAVE MADE LOVE TO A MAN"*

"Je ne fais l'amour qu'à Montréal."

ABOUT THE AUTHOR

Rabin Ramah was born in Trinidad to a large Roman Catholic family of both Indian and African ancestry. He immigrated with his family to Toronto, Canada, when he was a pre-teen. Geography has left an indelible stamp on Rabin's writing, as he has lived in Couva, Trinidad, Ottawa, Guelph, Vancouver, and his beloved Montréal.

Rabin has worked as a health educator for Men that have Sex with Men (MSM) at the Black Coalition for AIDS Prevention. He is a visual artist and a landscape and botanical photographer who now lives in Guelph, Ontario.

Lightning Source UK Ltd.
Milton Keynes UK
UKHW011831040621
384966UK00001B/49